P9-APO-287

BROWN

MY ALTER EGO IS A SUPERHERO
BOOK I

This is the first book in the series
My Alter Ego Is a Superhero

Enchanted Lion Books gratefully acknowledges the support of NORLA
for the translation and publication of this book.

HÅKON ØVREÅS

BROWN

Illustrated by
ØYVIND TORSETER

Translated from the Norwegian by Kari Dickson

ENCHANTED LION BOOKS
NEW YORK

On the day that his grandfather died, Rusty had to
spend the whole day with his Auntie Ranveig, as his
parents were busy at the hospital. Auntie Ranveig's
house smelled of liverwurst, and there were small glass
figurines everywhere: on the TV, on the shelves…
There was even a glass reindeer in the bathroom.
And she kept the radio on in the living room all day.

They had fish for dinner. Rusty sat and looked
down at his plate, at the heap of fried onions hiding
the fish. The fork felt heavy in his hand.

"Come on, eat your food," Auntie Ranveig said.
"Don't you like fish?"

1

"I like Swedish Fish," Rusty offered.

After dinner, his father came to pick him up.
That was when he told him that Grandpa had died.

"Okay," Rusty replied and put his jacket on.

He went out to the car. He sat there picking at
a sticker on the dashboard. After a while, his father
came out too. He got into the driver's seat and put
the key in the ignition, but didn't start the engine.

"Everything all right?" he asked.

"Everything's fine," Rusty said, his eyes glued to the white remains of the sticker.

Then his father started the car, and they drove home.

Rusty went to Auntie Ranveig's again the next day, as his parents had to go back to the hospital.

"Why?" Rusty asked.

"We have to sort out all the practicalities," his mother said.

Rusty nodded, as if he knew what "all the practicalities" meant.

When they had moved from town, his mother had said it was more practical to live in the country. At the time, he thought "practical" meant that he would see more of Grandpa, but he now realized that was wrong.

Auntie Ranveig was waiting at the door when he walked up the steps.

Rusty slipped past and took off his shoes.

"Hi, Rusty," she said and ruffled his hair. "Nice that you're going to be here again today!"

"Yes, I think it's practical," Rusty said.

He sat down on the sofa. There were three glass penguins on the coffee table in front of him. Auntie Ranveig went into the kitchen and began making a

racket with a machine. Rusty went to see what it was. She was standing by a large, electric meat grinder. After a while, she turned it off.

"We're going to have meatballs for supper," she announced. Rusty could see her snaggletooth when she smiled.

Rusty heard Auntie Ranveig clattering about with the plates and glasses. She called, "Can you go and get a bottle of juice from the cellar?"

"Okay!" Rusty called back.

He opened the door to the cellar. It smelled like a bag full of dirty gym clothes. He switched the light on and went down. The walls looked like an old, moldy dishcloth. He went over and pressed a bubble in the white paint. It flaked off. He went over to the shelf where the juice was and took down a bottle from the top. White flakes of dust swirled up, and Rusty had to cough. He turned around to go back up the stairs. And there, underneath, he spotted three large cans of paint. Rusty bent down. It was brown paint.

When they were eating dinner, Rusty asked, "Can I have the paint you've got stored under the stairs?"

Auntie Ranveig had just put a big meatball in her mouth. She looked at Rusty as she chewed.

"Why do you want the paint?" she asked after a while.

"To paint something," Rusty said.

"Watercolors are better for children," Auntie Ranveig said.

"But I want to paint the fort I'm building with my friend Jack."

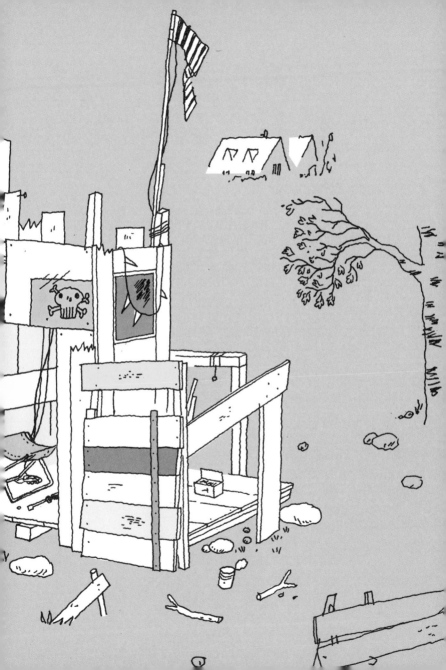

Rannveig looked at him for a long time, nodding.

"So, you've made a friend out here."

"Yes—Jack. And we're building a fort together."

"Ah, I see. Well, you can't paint a fort with watercolors."

"No," Rusty said.

"I'm sure you can have the paint," Auntie Ranveig said eventually, "but let's ask your father first."

Rusty stood by the window and waited for his parents' car to drive up to the house. Then he went down into the cellar and carried the three cans of paint over to the cellar door. He opened the door, carried one can out to the car, and put it in the trunk. Then he hurried back to get the others before closing the trunk as quietly as he could. When he came up from the cellar, Auntie Ranveig and his father were in the living room, talking.

"There you are," his father said. "Everything all right?"

"Yep," Rusty said.

"Have you been good?" his mother asked.

His father stretched out his hand as if there were something in it.

Rusty looked at him.

"We went to Grandpa's house and tidied up a bit. We thought you might like this."

His father opened his hand. In it was an old pocket watch. Rusty remembered it well. It used to hang on the end of a chain. He picked it up. The watch was still warm from his father's hand.

"It's stopped," Rusty said.

"Just needs winding up," his father said. He turned back to Auntie Ranveig. Rusty tried winding the crown, but there was still no ticking. And the hands didn't move either.

Jack's mailbox was skewed on its post, and his room was in the attic, so they had to climb up a ladder to reach it. From his window, they could see the church spire. Its top poked out from the silver-gray scaffolding that had been erected so the roof could be repaired.

"My grandpa died on Monday," Rusty said.

"Oh," Jack said. "My uncle died in the mountains. He fell down a crack in a glacier, and they couldn't get him out. So he's still down there in the ice, frozen solid. My dad says that when the ice melts, he'll come back to life."

"That's impossible," Rusty said.

"No, it's not. Ask my dad."

"Your uncle would be really confused when he woke up then, wouldn't he?" Rusty said.

He sat down and fiddled with a model airplane.

"By the way, I've got lots of paint for the fort," he said. "Brown paint."

"Oh," Jack said. "Well, my cousin works in a paint factory, so I can get as much paint as I want."

Rusty spun one of the wheels on the airplane. It fell off.

"Did you just break my plane?"

"No," Rusty said. "I can fix it."

"You'll have to pay for it."

"Is there any glue left?" Rusty asked.

"Glue's not free, you know," Jack said.

Rusty put the airplane down.

"Want to paint the fort?"

"Maybe tomorrow," Jack said. "I have to go to a meeting with my mom."

"What kind of meeting?"

"I dunno. But Mom says I have to go."

After he left Jack's, Rusty walked along the path at the back of the gardens and up to the forest. There were three bikes lying by the edge of the forest, close to where he and Jack had built the fort. Rusty looked up at the fort. There were three older boys there. He recognized them immediately as Anton, Ruben, and the minister's son. They always hung out together.

And now they were standing there kicking at the planks. The minister's son was pulling at the wood, and the whole fort rocked from side to side. Rusty stopped on the path, still some distance away, and shouted, "Leave our fort alone!"

The boys stopped and looked down at Rusty.

"What did you say, squirt?" Ruben asked.

"Leave our fort alone," Rusty said again. "It's ours."

"I don't see your name on it," the minister's son said.

"We built it, so it's ours."

"Well, it's our fort now," Anton said. And he laughed as he said it. "We need some planks."

Rusty looked at the bikes and then back up at the bullies by the fort.

"You have your names on these bikes?" he asked.

No one said anything. Rusty could feel his hands shaking. So no one would see, he balled them up as tight as he could.

"Well, I happen to need a bike, and since your names aren't on them, I'll just help myself."

Rusty reached for one of the bikes. The boys threw down the planks and took off down the hill.

"You wanna get your face smashed in?" the minister's son shouted.

Rusty dropped the bike and ran. When he got to the house where his classmate Lou lived, he dove into the hedge and pushed his way through the twisted branches. But he could still hear his pursuers behind him, so he ran across the garden, up the steps to Lou's door, and rang the bell. Anton came up behind him and grabbed his arm, but just then the door opened, and Lou's mother appeared in front of them. Anton let go and retreated back down the steps.

"Hi, Rusty," Lou's mother said, smiling. She was wearing a blue shawl over her shoulders. "Have you come to see Lou?"

Rusty went into the hallway. He closed the door behind him. When he looked out of the window, he could see the boys on the road outside.

"Lou!" her mother called up the stairs. "You've got
a visitor!"

Her mother turned back to Rusty.

"She'll be down in a minute." She went into the
living room.

Lou came down the stairs. She looked at Rusty like
he was an alien.

"The minister's son was chasing me."

"Come in then."

They went into the kitchen. From the window they
could see the boys hanging around on the road. They

had gone back to get their bikes and were circling in front of the house.

"I don't know how I'm going to get home," Rusty said.

"Let's go up to my room. Eventually, they'll get bored out there."

Lou's room smelled of hairspray. She had horse posters on the wall.

"Do you like horses?" Rusty asked.

"No, not really. But my sister didn't want them anymore, and she thought I might get interested if I looked at them long enough."

"Has it worked?"

"Don't know yet. I'll try for another month."

"My grandpa died on Monday," Rusty said.

"Oh, that's too bad," Lou said. "My granny died last year, but she wasn't very nice, so I wasn't sad. Are you sad?"

"No, but Grandpa was really, really nice."

"I don't understand why you're not sad then."

"Why wasn't your granny nice?"

"We were never allowed into her house, so we
had to sit on the steps when Mom went to visit.
And when she came to our house, we had to curtsy,
and we weren't allowed to say, 'What?' We had to
say, 'Pardon?' instead. And we weren't allowed into the
living room, because we made too much noise,
and one Christmas, she gave us a book about etiquette,
and once, my sister forgot to put her napkin on her
lap before the meal, so she didn't get any food and
was sent to bed early. Granny was crazy."

"Didn't your mom say anything?"

"Don't think she dared, because Granny was
so crazy."

"Grandpa wasn't crazy at all."

"Then I don't understand why you're not sad,"
Lou said.

The boys had disappeared from the road by the time
Rusty left. Lou stood on the steps and waved. Rusty
thought he heard bike tires behind him and started
to run.

His mother and father were sitting in the kitchen when he got home. There was a pot on the table. He saw from their plates that they had already eaten.

"Where have you been?" his mother asked.

"I was at Jack's," Rusty said.

"I called Jack's house, but you weren't there," his mother said.

"I had to hide from three boys."

"Hide? Have you been getting into trouble? I don't want you getting into trouble, Rusty. We're new here, and it's not good if you're getting into trouble already."

"We've been here for six months now," his father said.

"It wasn't my fault," Rusty said. "They were pulling down the fort that Jack and I built."

"I see," his mother said. "But still, it's not good to get into trouble."

Rusty didn't say anything more. He put a potato on his plate, held it with one hand, and peeled off the soft skin with a knife. His mother got up, put her plate in the sink, and left the kitchen. His father sat there looking at Rusty.

"Everything all right, Rusty?" he asked.

"Everything's fine," Rusty said.

That evening, there was a movie on TV. It was about a superhero called Ray-X, who could see through houses and cars. This time, he had to stop the evil villain from pulling down an apartment building. Rusty had heard people talking about the movie at school.

"Time for bed," his mother said just as the movie was about to start.

"Can I watch the movie?" Rusty asked.

"Yes, that's fine," said his father.

"Oh, it's far too late," said his mother.

Rusty stayed put. At the commercial break, his mother told him that now he really had to go to bed. Rusty didn't say anything, but got up when they heard

noise from outside. It sounded like someone shouting.
Rusty pressed his face up against the window. He
could see three dark shadows in the garden.

"Our apple tree!" his mother cried.

His father jumped up and ran to the veranda
door. He slipped on a pair of clogs and went out.
The shadows disappeared over the hedge. Rusty
rushed to the front door. He stood on the step and
peered into the dark. All was quiet. Rusty felt the cold
air on his arms. Then he heard some other sounds.
Three shadows sped past them down the road. It was
completely dark, but still easy enough to recognize
Ruben's high handlebars.

"Punks!" his father said when Rusty came back
inside. "A shame I didn't get my hands on them!"

"I don't want anyone bothering us," his mother said.

The movie was on again, and Rusty got to watch a
bit more. Until the next commercial break.

Rusty lay in bed, but his eyes were wide open.
He heard a bike braking on the gravel outside and
thought he heard laughter as well. But when he got

out of bed and looked down at the road, it was dark and empty. Rusty climbed back into bed. He picked up his grandpa's pocket watch and lay there winding it, but it still didn't start to tick. Every time he felt his eyelids getting heavy, he thought he heard bikes outside and someone shouting and laughing.

He heard his parents go to bed.

He switched the light on as quietly as he could and crept over to the closet. The three cans of paint that he had taken from Auntie Ranveig were at the back. He opened one of the cans and dipped a pencil into the paint. The thick brown mass was so heavy to stir that he could write letters in it. He started to write his name: R-U-S-T-Y. The paint settled back into place. Then he wrote B-R-O-W-N. The surface of the paint leveled out again.

R-U-S-T-Y-B-R-O-W-N.

He stared at the letters as they slowly sank back into the paint. Then he wrote them again: R-U-S-T-Y-B-R-O-W-N.

Standing up abruptly, he pulled some brown pants from a shelf and found a black-and-brown striped

T-shirt on the shelf above. He tiptoed out into the
living room. There was a light-brown throw-blanket
on the sofa. Rusty took it back into his room and tied
it in a knot around his neck. It made a great cape,
but the knot was too big. Rusty took some scissors
from his desk drawer. He cut out a half-moon to fit
around his neck. Now the cape was perfect. He used
the piece of material he had cut out to make a mask.
A superhero mask.

Rusty tiptoed out into the bathroom to look at himself in the mirror. There he was: Brown the Superhero. His heart hammered under his brown disguise. He was no longer just Rusty. He was Brown. His mother's brown belt was hanging over a cabinet door. The perfect superhero belt. With it on, he was ready for action. He went back into his room and took Grandpa's pocket watch out from under his pillow. He was just about to put it in his pocket when he noticed

that the second hand was moving! Brown put the watch to his ear and heard it ticking. Then he put the watch in his pocket and attached the chain to his belt.

Brown picked up one of the cans of paint and tiptoed as quietly as he could to the front door. He put on his shoes, opened the door, and crept out. The air was cold, and the wind tugged at his cape. The garage door was open, and Brown found a thick brush on one of the shelves at the back. Soon, he was running across

the road to the path on the other side. He knew where
Ruben lived—not far from Jack's.

Ruben's bike lay on the lawn in front of his house.
Brown crept up to the bike, flipped the lid off the can,
and dipped the brush into the paint. It clung to the
bristles in a great, fat blob. Then, slowly, he started
to spread the brown paint all over Ruben's bike.
Nice and brown, he thought. *I can just imagine how
happy he'll be when he discovers he's got a nice brown*

bike. Brown chuckled and wiped the brush off on the grass.

When he'd finished, Brown crept back out to the road and took off running, his cape flying behind.

He followed the path along the edge of the forest. It was dark under the trees, but Brown wasn't afraid. *Superheroes aren't afraid of the dark*, he told himself as he ran past the trees.

He wasn't far from home now. He was already at the big rock that he liked to climb, which sat where the footpath ended and the road began. But now, someone was sitting on the rock. Brown got a fright when he noticed, but was too close to run without being seen. It was an old man.

"Hi, Rusty," the man said. "I see you're on a mission."

Brown edged closer.

"Grandpa? Is that you?"

"Of course it's me. I'm just sitting here enjoying the nice summer's night."

"But … aren't you dead?"

"Yep," Grandpa said.

"How can you be sitting here then?"

"What about you?" Grandpa said. "Aren't you asleep in bed?"

"Um…yes," Brown said, hesitating. "I mean, Rusty is asleep in bed. I'm Brown."

Grandpa laughed and nodded.

"I understand," he said. "In which case, Grandpa is dead, and I'm Brownpa."

Brown sniggered.

"What are you doing with the paint?" Grandpa asked.

"Well, I…was going to paint something."

"That's my boy. But you better get on home now before your parents discover you're out and about in the middle of the night."

"Will I see you again, Grandpa?"

"Yes, of course you will. I sit here every now and then. I can see your house from here, and at the same time, I can look down to the water. And I can remember the times I went fishing there. Once, I

36

caught a huge pike that was almost as big as the boat.
Did I ever tell you about that?"

"No," Brown lied. "You've never told me that story."

"Or did I tell you about the time that I drove my vintage car down to Italy to buy a hotdog? Surely I've told you that story, haven't I?"

"No," Brown said. "Tell me!"

Grandpa looked at him for a long time. He laughed a little.

"Another night perhaps. You have to get yourself home now. The sun will be peeping over the hills soon."

Brown started to walk towards the house.

"See you tomorrow night," he called.

Grandpa waved from the rock.

When Brown was back in his room, he took off his disguise and was Rusty once again. He unhooked the watch from the belt. The hands had stopped. Rusty tried to wind it up, but nothing happened. Soon, he was back in bed, trying hard to fall asleep. As for his Brown disguise and the paint can, they were well-hidden at the back of the closet.

Jack and Rusty stood looking at the remains of their fort. Planks were scattered everywhere. Jack picked up the handle they had used for the front door.

"They did it just to be mean," Rusty said. "I asked them not to, but they went totally berserk and chased me away."

"I was once chased by ten boys. But I got away and called the army," said Jack. "And they sent fighter planes and tanks and arrested them all."

"Who were they?"

"It was a long time ago. They don't live around here anymore."

"But the army can't arrest people, can it?"

"Yes, it can," Jack said. "Haven't you heard of the military police? They come with tanks and guns when the police can't."

"I've never heard that," Rusty said.

"Ask my dad. It's true. I even got to sit in one of the tanks. I've got a photo of it at home to prove it."

Rusty said nothing. He picked up some planks and stacked them against the tree where they had built the fort. He looked at his hand. There were some flecks of brown paint on it.

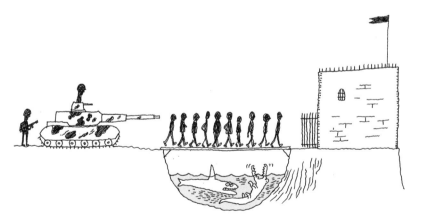

"Well, they got what they deserved," Rusty said.

"Who did?"

"The dopes who destroyed our fort and chased me all day. They got what they deserved."

"Did you call the army?"

"No," Rusty said. "I got help from a superhero."

"A superhero?" Jack laughed. "That's so dumb. I mean, did Ray-X come and beat them up?"

"Not Ray-X," Rusty said.

"Who then?"

"A new superhero you've never heard of."

"What he's called?"

Jack's grin was even broader.

"Brown."

Jack started laughing so hard that he collapsed, clutching his stomach.

"Brown?" he spluttered. "What's this guy's superpower?"

"He paints things brown."

Jack was unable to answer, because now he was lying on his back, laughing uncontrollably.

The laughter just rolled out of him. Rusty sat down next to Jack, and soon, he was convulsing too. Jack's laughter was contagious. When they finally managed to stop, Rusty said, "I was just kidding."

Jack had to go home, so Rusty headed home, too. He stood for a while looking at the rock where his grandpa had been sitting the night before. *It looks emptier than ever*, Rusty thought.

Anton, Ruben, and the minister's son were hanging around outside his house with their bikes. Ruben, who was pointing at his now-brown bicycle, was talking with Rusty's father on the front step.

"Nonsense," he heard his father say to the boys. "Rusty was home fast asleep last night. And where would he have gotten brown paint from, anyway?"

"But who else would have done it?" said the minister's son.

"Hi, Rusty," his father said as he walked up. "These boys are saying that you painted Ruben's bike brown. Do you know anything about it?"

"That's weird," Rusty said, hiding the hand with paint flecks on it in his pocket.

"We know you did it," Anton said. "You did it to take revenge because we wrecked your fort!"

"You destroyed Rusty's fort?" his father asked.

The boys fell silent. They looked sideways at each other.

"Now you leave Rusty alone," his father said angrily. "He's done nothing to any of you, and he certainly didn't paint any bikes last night. It's just ridiculous, you coming here and accusing Rusty when you pulled down the fort that he and Jack built."

The boys didn't answer. They left quickly, pushing their bikes. Rusty's father patted him on the shoulder, and they went inside. His mother was sitting in the kitchen.

"I don't like those boys," she said. A tear ran down her cheek. "I told you to stay away from them."

"Everything all right, Rusty?" his father asked.

"Everything's fine," Rusty said. He went upstairs to his room and closed the door.

After dinner, the doorbell rang. A stranger was
standing on the step when Rusty opened the door.
He was wearing a suit and held a briefcase. He wore
a strange smile. Rusty thought it looked like he was
laughing and crying at the same time.

"It's the man from the funeral home," his father said.

"Okay," Rusty said.

Rusty stood in the doorway to the living room
while the others sat around the table and talked. The
man from the funeral home spoke in a very quiet voice
and used lots of long, boring words. He had almost no

hair on the top of his head. The light from the ceiling lamp reflected on his shiny bald patch.

"You also have to decide what you want to say on the stone," the man said.

He took out a catalogue with photographs of gravestones and coffins.

"Do you know that he used to be a captain?" said Rusty's mother.

"Indeed." The man sat there nodding.

"He was away a lot when I was little, but always came back with a present for me. Jewelry, funny wooden figures—stuff like that. Once, I even got a peacock feather. No one else had one. But the strangest thing he brought home was a dried giraffe ear. He kept it wrapped up in paper in his office and would take it out on New Year's Eve. We would whisper our wishes for the coming year into the ear. He told us that the giraffe's ear had unimaginable powers and that all our wishes would come true."

Rusty's mother laughed. The man from the funeral home just kept nodding the whole time.

"Where's the ear now?" Rusty asked.

"Goodness, I don't know," his mother said. "I didn't find it when we were going through Grandpa's things."

It was late in the evening before the man from the funeral home left. Rusty went to brush his teeth.

"Have you seen my brown belt, Rusty?" his mother asked.

Rusty looked at his mother as he brushed his teeth. He gurgled a little so she would see he couldn't answer.

"I can't find my brown belt," she said. "I thought I left it hanging in here."

Rusty brushed and rinsed for a very long time, only finishing once his mother had left. Then he went into his room. The belt was lying right at the back of the closet. There were some specks of paint on it. Rusty tried to scrape them off with his nail, but it didn't work. When he heard someone out in the hall, he quickly put the belt away. Soon after, his father came in to say goodnight.

When his father had gone, Rusty looked at the watch. The hands weren't moving. He held it to his ear. He thought he heard something, a faint creaking. Keeping the watch next to his ear, he put his head down on the pillow.

Rusty was eating breakfast when he heard the crunch of bicycle tires on the gravel outside. His mother looked out of the window.

"It's those boys again," she said.

He looked out and saw the minister's son coming up to ring the doorbell. His father opened the door. Rusty got up, went out into the hall, and stood just behind him.

"Rusty's been at it again," Anton said.

"Yeah," said the minister's son.

"Look," Ruben said.

He pointed at Anton's bike. It had been painted black.

"It's black," Rusty said. "Not brown."

"What do you mean?" his father said, looking down at him.

"Someone has painted the bike black," Rusty said.

Rusty's father looked at him, then at the bike. It was propped up on its kickstand in the middle of the driveway, the black paint gleaming.

"Were you boys in our apple tree the other day?" his father asked.

The boys didn't answer.

"Well, Rusty certainly didn't paint your bike black," he continued, looking at Anton.

The boys muttered something and stood there for a while, kicking at the gravel, before pushing their bikes off.

"Strange," Rusty's father said quietly. "Very strange."

His mother was sitting at the table. She had tears in her eyes.

"It's just boys playing pranks," his father said. "Nothing to do with us."

54

Rusty finished his breakfast before slipping on his shoes and running out.

Jack was at the top of the hill. He had a hammer in his hand and had already fixed the frame of the fort.

"We'll rebuild it," he said. "Just a hundred times better. When my dad was little, he built a fort that was thirty feet high—higher than the church spire. And when they stood at the top, they could see all the way to the next town."

"That's impossible," Rusty mumbled.

"It's a fact," Jack said. "Just ask my dad."

Rusty picked up a plank and carried it over to Jack.

"You should have seen Anton's bike," Rusty said. "They came by this morning. Said I'd painted the bike black."

Jack snorted.

"Really?" he said.

Rusty stopped dead in his tracks and looked intensely at Jack before saying, "Do you know anything about it?"

"Nope, not a thing," Jack said. "All I know is that

they were outside our house yesterday, and when my mom came home in the car, they wouldn't move their bikes out of the way. Mom tried to tell them off, but the jerks just stood there laughing. Later, when it was dark, a firecracker exploded in our mailbox. I was so mad that I…"

"You what?" Rusty asked.

Jack hammered in a nail.

"That I got some help. You know, I called in a superhero."

"A superhero?" Rusty said and started to giggle.

"Yeah, I don't think you know him. He's called Black."

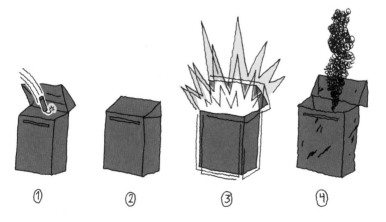

Jack was laughing so hard he dropped the hammer. Rusty collapsed, too.

"And you didn't believe in Brown," he giggled.

"That was before I saw the brown bike," said Jack.

"Brown and Black," Rusty said. "The Guardians of the Fort." They cracked up again.

Eventually, they got back to work. But it wasn't long before they heard the screech of bikes braking at the bottom of the hill.

And there on the path were Anton, Ruben, and the minister's son with the black and brown bikes.

"We know you did this!" the minister's son shouted. He got off his bike and came up the hill toward Rusty and Jack. "We know it."

"Yeah, we know it," Anton and Ruben repeated. They came up the hill toward the fort.

Ruben started to kick the frame that Jack had rebuilt.

"Back off," Jack said. "It's got nothing to do with us."

"We know you did it," said the minister's son. And he gave the frame a great big shove. They heard a crack, and suddenly, the fort looked like bird's nest again.

Jack grabbed the hammer and hit the minister's son squarely on the back. He howled and fell to the ground, where he lay writhing.

"Oops," Jack said. He dropped the hammer and took a few steps back.

"I'm going to get you!" the minister's son shouted.

"Get him!" Ruben growled.

But before the minister's son had even raised his arm, Rusty and Jack had started to run. They were halfway down the path, and Rusty could still hear the bullies shouting behind them. Rusty dove through Lou's hedge.

"In here!" Rusty shouted and grabbed Jack by the arm.

Quick as a flash, they were up the steps and pressing on the bell. They could hear their pursuers shouting behind the house.

Lou's mother opened the door. "Oh, how nice to see you! Come inside," she said when she saw Rusty. "And Jack too! I'll call for Lou."

As the door shut behind them, they saw the boys through the window, running around the corner to the front of the house. Anton ran down to the road, while the minister's son and Ruben held back, looking around. Rusty and Jack retreated farther down the hall. They could hear the boys on the gravel outside. Lou came skipping down the stairs with a big smile.

"Are the boys after you again?" she asked.

The doorbell rang.

"Don't tell them we're here," Rusty said.

When Lou opened the door, Rusty and Jack hid at the end of hall.

"Can we talk to Jack?" they heard the minister's son say.

"And Rusty," Ruben said.

"They're not here," Lou told them.

"We know they are," Anton said.

"Well, I haven't seen them."

"I can see their shoes," said the minister's son.

"Oh, those are my dad's shoes," Lou said.

"You're hiding them," Anton said. "We just want to talk to them."

"Yeah, we just want to talk to them," Ruben repeated.

"They're not here," Lou said and shut the front door quickly, locking it.

Rusty and Jack took off their shoes, and they all went into the kitchen. From the window, they could

see the boys hanging around outside. Ruben picked up
some gravel and threw a piece at the window.

"Mom!" Lou shouted. "Some boys outside are
throwing gravel at the window."

Lou's mother went out onto the step. From the
window, they could see the boys slouch away.

"Let's go up to my room," Lou said.

Jack and Rusty installed themselves in Lou's room. The smell of hairspray wasn't as strong this time.

It smells more like a meadow, Rusty thought.

"Do you like horses?" Jack asked.

"No, she doesn't really," Rusty said.

Jack looked at Rusty, confused.

"Why are those boys always chasing you?" Lou asked.

"Don't know," Rusty said.

Jack shook his head. "They've always been trouble. Like that time when the minister's son set fire to a tree on the hill behind school."

"They say we've painted their bikes," Rusty said. "One brown and one black."

"Painted their bikes?" Lou sounded surprised. "Why would you do that?"

"Don't know," Jack said.

Rusty shook his head. "Me neither," he said.

"Strange," Lou said.

"I think a couple of superheroes did it," Rusty said.

Jack glared at him.

"Superheroes?" Lou said.

"Yeah, well, that's what I think. Superheroes who like to paint."

"Right…" Lou said. "And you know these superheroes?"

Jack stared at Rusty hard and shook his head.

"Nah, but it's possible I might have heard their names," Rusty said.

Jack shrugged.

"What are they called then?" Lou asked.

"Umm…" Rusty hesitated.

"I don't think Lou wants to hear about your crazy dreams," Jack said.

"Yes, I do."

"I think one is called Brown. He only paints stuff brown."

"Brown?" Lou laughed. "You're joking."

"And there's one who uses only black paint…"

"Rusty…" Jack warned.

Rusty hesitated.

"Come on, tell me," Lou said. "I won't tell anyone."

"Fine," Jack said. "The one who paints things black is called … well … Black."

Lou laughed again, a happy laugh. It reminded Rusty of a horse neighing.

"Are there any more superheroes?" Lou asked when she had stopped laughing.

"Nah, I don't think so," Rusty said.

"Is there room for another one?"

"Maybe," Rusty said. "If those jerks don't stop chasing us."

Jack nodded.

"Together, they're called the Guardians of the Fort," Jack explained. "And I'm pretty sure they're going to meet at midnight tonight, up by the fort. If you know any superheroes, you could tell them."

Lou nodded gravely.

That evening, the phone rang. Rusty could tell something was wrong from the way his father was talking. His father glanced over at him, and a shiver ran down his spine. He got up from the sofa and went to his room. There, he took out his grandpa's watch and held it tight. The hands weren't moving.

A few minutes later, there was a knock at the door. His father popped his head inside.

"Can I talk to you, Rusty?"

Rusty nodded.

"Is everything all right?"

"Everything's fine," Rusty said.

"I've just been speaking to the minister," his father said.

"Okay," Rusty said.

"Those boys have been bothering you, haven't they? It seems Lou's mother went to talk to him."

"That's good," Rusty said.

"But I agree with the minister: It's very odd that those bikes have been painted. Don't you think?"

Rusty shrugged.

"Do you know anything about it, Rusty?"

Rusty rubbed the watch. It was warm in the palm of his hand.

"It's a little strange," Rusty said.

"Yes, actually, it is. The minister told me that Anton's and Ruben's parents are thinking of calling the police."

Rusty felt his insides turn to ice. His hand—the one not clutching the watch—was shaking.

"You mean the army?" he asked.

His father laughed.

"No, why? The army isn't the police," his father said, mussing Rusty's hair.

"Haven't you heard of the military police?" Rusty asked.

"Yes, of course. They do exist," his father said. "But I think the minister meant just the normal, ordinary police. He wasn't sure, but he didn't think they'd done anything yet."

"Okay," Rusty said.

Rusty felt tired, but now he was unable to sleep.
He sat in bed and held the watch tight. The hands still
wouldn't budge. Rusty got out of bed, went over to the
window, and looked out at the empty road. Everything
was dark and quiet. When he got back into bed and
sat there, he felt his eyelids getting heavy. But he jerked
awake when he thought he heard bicycle tires sliding
on the gravel, and police sirens in the distance. He
rubbed his eyes and tried to hold his breath so he could
listen better, but then the sounds disappeared.

He sat in bed looking down at his watch. Suddenly,
he saw the second hand begin to move. Then, slowly,
the minute hand started to move, too. Rusty looked

over at the clock radio on his bedside table.
It was exactly midnight.

Rusty got up, his mind racing. *It's superhero time!* he thought. He dug his Brown costume out of the closet, put on his mask, fastened his belt, and tied on his cape. He was Brown once more. Seconds later, he was standing on the front step with a can of paint in his hand. He ran across the road, past the big rock, and headed down the path along the back of the gardens. He almost tripped on some roots, but was soon up the hill where the remains of the fort

lay scattered. He looked out over the rooftops. Not a sound to be heard. But then, something crunched behind him. He spun around. A shadow disappeared behind a bush.

"Who's there?" Brown called out.

No one answered. Brown drew closer. Something was stirring behind the bush.

"Who's there?" he called again.

A shadow slowly emerged. Brown could just make out a face with a black mask, and a black cape on the shadow's back.

"It's Black," the shadow said.

"Brown here," said Brown.

"Guardians of the Fort," Black said. "What's our mission for tonight?"

"The minister's son's bike still hasn't been painted," Brown whispered.

Just then, something snapped behind them in the forest. They dived behind the bush, from where they could see a figure coming up the hill with a cape fluttering behind.

"Reporting for duty," whispered a reedy voice.

"Who are you?" Brown whispered.

"I'm Blue, or the Blue Avenger."

"We greet you, Blue," said Brown.

"Yeah," said Black. "That's it! Let's paint the minister's son's bike blue!"

"But I couldn't find any paint," Blue said. "I just wanted to be part of this. I've got a brush with me though."

"Well, we'll have to paint it brown *and* black," Brown said.

Soon, the three superheroes were running down to the house next to the churchyard. They rounded the corner of the large garage and saw that there was still

light in the windows. The minister's son's bike was standing at the bottom of the steps. Brown and Black flipped open their cans of paint, while Blue held a brush at the ready. Together, they tiptoed over the gravel. Suddenly, the outdoor light came on. Brown, Black, and Blue froze. They heard a noise at the front door and jumped behind a bush. The door opened. The minister came out onto the front step. He peered into the dark, looking straight towards the superheroes, who were now hiding behind a bush. Not seeing them, he went back inside. Soon after, the light went off.

"Let's try again," Black said.

They crept along the edge of the lawn.

"We'll have to move the bike away from the steps," Blue whispered.

But just as they reached the corner of the house, the outdoor light came on again. The door opened again. And the minister came out again. This time, he had a flashlight with him, and he shone it on the bush where they had hidden before. He came down the steps and walked around a little. Brown, Black, and Blue pressed themselves flat against the wall around the corner and watched the flashlight beam sweep over the dark lawn, coming close, then disappearing again. Black peeked around the corner.

"He's pushing the bike into the garage," he whispered.

"Darn," said Blue.

"He's locking the door."

"Double darn," said Blue.

Black jumped back as the beam from the flashlight hit his mask.

"Retreat!" he whispered. "Fast!"

Back at the fort, the three out-of-breath superheroes sat whispering and laughing in the dark.

"Shame about the bike. How are we going to paint it now?" Blue whispered.

"If it hadn't been for the stupid minister," Black said.

"Maybe we should have painted his face," Blue laughed.

"Or painted his cars," Black suggested. "Apparently, he's got two vintage cars in the garage. Him and his son are crazy about cars."

"Grandpa has a vintage car in his garage, too," Brown said.

"Maybe you'll inherit it!" Blue exclaimed.

Brown hurried to add, "I mean, Rusty's grandpa, he's…a friend of mine."

"Well, if Rusty inherits the car, he'll make the minister's son so jealous he'll turn green!"

Black and Blue laughed while Brown stood there thinking.

"What about the church spire?" he blurted out. "We could paint the church spire black and brown!"

Black and Blue looked at him.

"It's impossible. It's too high," Black said.

"They haven't taken down the scaffolding yet," Blue said. "They put it up so they could fix the roof."

"Exactly," Brown said.

"I'd forgotten about that," Black said.

"But it's still not possible," Blue said. "We don't have enough paint. We should have had some cans of blue paint."

"Blue paint!" Brown suddenly remembered. "I know where there's blue paint! There's loads of it in Grandpa's garage behind the old car. They were going to paint the house this summer."

"That's great!" Blue said.

"Yeah, Rusty's grandpa, that is…" Brown said.

"But do you think we can take it?" Blue asked.

"I'm not sure," Brown said. "They might notice."

"No one would notice if we borrowed a can, would they?" Black said.

"No!" Blue exclaimed. "And then we can paint the church spire!"

"Are you sure it's a good idea?" Brown asked.

Black and Blue looked at him.

"Of course it's a good idea!" they said. "It was your idea!"

Before calling it a night, the three superheroes hatched their next plan. After, Brown sprinted along the path home. As he neared the rock, he saw that his grandpa was sitting there again.

"You're out on another mission, I see," Grandpa said.

"It wasn't so successful this time," Brown said.

"Have you got yourself into trouble?" Grandpa asked.

"I think so," Brown said.

"That's my boy," Grandpa said. "How else would anything ever get done?"

"Could I borrow that paint in your garage?" Brown asked.

"The cans of blue paint?" Grandpa laughed. "Yes, take them."

"Thank you," Brown said.

"But make sure that no one finds out. There's a key behind the woodpile that nobody else knows about."

Brown nodded.

"You know, you've got a gravestone," Brown said.

"Already?" Grandpa said. "I haven't even been buried yet!"

"A man came to see us, and we had to look through a catalogue."

"A catalogue?" Grandpa snorted. "You see that hill on the other side of the water?" Grandpa pointed. "That's my gravestone. Anything else is simply too small."

Brown smiled.

"Do you remember how strong I am?" Grandpa asked.

Brown nodded.

"I once lifted a big tree trunk. Did I ever tell you about that? When my dog got one of its paws stuck, and I had to save it?"

Grandpa put his hand on his bicep and flexed his arm.

"It's a shame, really, that they're going to bury someone with such good, big muscles."

"What's it like being dead, Grandpa?"

"Pretty much like everything else, I guess."

"What do you mean?"

"Well," Grandpa said. He took something wrapped in paper out of his pocket. "I've experienced so many strange and wonderful things that I thought it might be nice to relax for a little while. To just wander around and make sure that the sun is glittering on the water in the morning, and that the leaves on the trees are turning yellow, and that it rains every now and then."

Grandpa unwrapped the paper. Inside was the dried giraffe's ear. It was yellow and brown, and the fur was worn in a few places.

"You know that the giraffe has special powers?" Grandpa said. He held the ear out to Brown.

"If you get into trouble again, you'll be able to fix things. Just whisper what you want to happen into the giraffe's ear, then wait and see. Everything will sort itself out. If you've got a giraffe's ear, things always turn out all right."

Brown ran his finger over the ear. The fur was hard and smelled of strange spices and old attics.

"Now, you'd better get home to bed before your parents notice you're missing."

Brown said goodbye to Grandpa and sprinted across the road toward home.

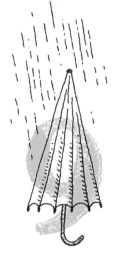

The day that Grandpa was to be buried, it rained. Rusty stood on the front step and watched the raindrops burst on the gravel. There was a small explosion every time one landed. He fidgeted in his black suit. Grandpa's watch was in his pocket. Rusty took it out and looked at it. His father came out onto the front step and opened an umbrella. He said nothing, just nodded to Rusty, and they walked to the car together. Rusty got into the back. Soon after, his mother came down the steps protected by a big black umbrella. She got into the car before she closed first

the umbrella and then the door. Her face was pale
and empty.

Rusty thought the church looked like it was leaning
against the scaffolding for support. *Like it's using
a crutch*, he mused. It was icy cold inside, and a big
white coffin stood in the aisle. There were flowers
everywhere, and sad music flooded from the organ.
The minister was up at the front by the altar, talking to
a big man with a bowtie. When he saw Rusty's mother
and father, he went up to them and shook their hands.

"My condolences," he said, and nodded. Rusty noticed that he had a wart over his right eyebrow.

After he had shaken hands with Rusty's parents, he bent down and took Rusty by the hand.

"My condolences," he said. Rusty nodded, as he had seen his father do. The minister stiffened. His eyes were glued to Rusty's hand. A fleck of paint! Rusty hadn't managed to wash it off. The minister said nothing, just raised his eyes and squinted into Rusty's face. Rusty felt how hot and red his cheeks were. He stood there staring at the minister's wart. There was a black hair sprouting out of it. And it was curly, like a pig's tail. The minister still wouldn't let go of his hand; he just stood there staring at it. Rusty tried to pull free, but the minister would not let go. Finally, Rusty's father coughed, and it was as if the spell was broken. The minister nodded, dropped Rusty's hand, and walked back to the altar.

"How strange," his father whispered.

"Not now," his mother whispered back.

Rusty saw that the minister was talking to the man in the bowtie again. They both looked to where Rusty and his parents were sitting. The man nodded. Rusty shuddered.

"Yes, it's cold in here," his mother said, rubbing his back.

Rusty sat, clutching the watch tight in his hand.

When they stood by the grave, the rain was even heavier than before. His mother held her hand to her face, and her whole body was shaking. His father looked tired. Rusty stood close to his father under the umbrella. The minister picked up a small spade and threw some earth onto the white coffin. When he had finished, everyone came over to Rusty's mother and father and shook their hands. They also held their hands out to Rusty. But Rusty hid his hand in his pocket and retreated behind his father. The last person to come up to shake their hands was the minister. But Rusty went over to Auntie Ranveig before the minister could get to him. Auntie Ranveig put her arm around him, and they walked slowly towards the car.

"How do you wash off paint?" Rusty asked.

"Why are you asking about that now?" Auntie Ranveig said.

"I was just wondering, and Mom and Dad are so sad," Rusty said. "Jack and I are going to paint the fort, but we're worried we might make a mess."

"You use paint thinner, but you'll have to ask your father first," she said.

94

"Okay, I will," Rusty said.

They stood and waited by the car. His parents arrived soon after.

"Everything all right, Rusty?" his father asked.

"Everything's fine," Rusty said.

They got into the car. His mother blew her nose with a hanky.

"I don't understand why the minister had to bring those bikes up again today," she said. "There must be something wrong with him."

She started to sob.

"He's quite a character," Rusty's father said. He looked back at Rusty before starting the car and turning out of the parking lot.

There was a bottle of paint thinner in the garage. When Rusty unscrewed the top, the strong smell hit him. He poured a little onto a rag and rubbed at the fleck of paint. Soon, it was gone. Rusty heaved a sigh of relief, put the bottle back on the shelf, and went into the house. Auntie Ranveig and his mother were sitting in the living room. There was a plate of sandwiches on the table. Rusty went into the bathroom and washed

off the smell of the paint thinner. Then he went out and had a sandwich.

When Auntie Ranveig had gone, his mother went into the kitchen to put away the sandwiches. Rusty stayed where he was in the living room. His father stayed, too.

"The minister wanted us to ask you if you know who painted the bikes."

"But you already have," Rusty said.

"He wanted me to ask you again," his father said. "I told him that you didn't know anything. That's the truth, isn't it?"

Rusty nodded. He felt cold.

"He said that you have brown paint on your hand."

"Me?" Rusty said. "Brown paint?"

"I said that couldn't be right. But can I see your hands, just to be sure?"

"Just to be sure?"

"Yes, so I'm not lying to the minister. You can understand that, can't you?"

Rusty held out his hands.

"There," he said, angrily. "Hope you're satisfied."

His father didn't say anything. Outraged, Rusty got up and stormed off to his room, slamming the door behind him. He sat down on the bed. He could feel his heart racing. Taking the watch out of his jacket pocket, he held it tight. The hands weren't moving. He lay back against the pillow. His father knocked on the door.

"I'm sleeping," Rusty said.

Rusty got up, took off his suit, and crawled under the covers. He laid the watch beside the pillow.

When he woke up, the room was pitch black and the watch was ticking faintly. The hands were moving slowly, tick by tick. Rusty got up and went over to the window. All was quiet. He crept over to the closet and put on his disguise. He opened the door to the hall and tiptoed out. The house was still.

His grandpa's rock by the path was empty. It was still wet from the rain. Brown continued on to Grandpa's house. Blue and Black were already there, waiting on the steps. They were laughing.

"There you are at last," Black said.

"Why did we meet here?" Blue asked.

"How long have you been sitting here chatting?" Brown asked.

"Lou's been telling me about her crazy granny," Black laughed. "She's completely bonkers."

"It was Blue who told you," Blue said. "Not Lou."

"True, true," Black said. "But her gran is hilarious."

They found the key behind the woodpile, where Rusty's grandpa had told him it would be. But when Brown went to unlock the garage door, he discovered it was already open.

"How strange!" Brown said.

"Maybe some thieves have been here," Blue whispered.

They crept into the garage. Grandpa's old vintage car was there. It was dusty.

"If only we could drive around in that," Black said and rubbed some dust off one of the headlights. "I bet the minister's son would be pretty jealous."

"Grandpa said it was fine to take the paint," Brown said.

"Isn't he dead?" Blue asked.

"Well…he would have said it was fine," Brown corrected himself.

There was only one can of paint behind the car.

"There should be lots more paint here," Brown said.

They took the can of blue paint and headed off into the night, walking one behind the other. They went past the fort so they wouldn't be seen on the road. At the top of the hill, they perched together on a plank, looking out at the houses and the silhouette of the church spire.

"I was in church today, and the minister caught me," Brown said. "He saw that I had paint on my hand."

The others looked at him.

"Then he knows it's you," Blue said.

"Then he knows it was us who did it," Black said.

"I know," Brown said. "Maybe it would be stupid to paint the church spire tonight."

"We have to paint it blue," Blue said.

"But he knows it's us," Brown said.

"You could just say that he was seeing things," Black said. "He's a minister, after all. There's loads about people having visions in the Bible."

"Have you read the Bible?" Blue asked.

"No, but I've heard people talk about it," Black said. "I have to go with my mom to these meetings where they talk about people in the Bible having visions and doing miraculous things before they die and go to paradise. I think they're full of it, but the minister has to believe it."

"My granny read the Bible every day," Blue said. "I think that's why she was so crazy. But my mom says she would've been even crazier if she hadn't read the Bible. Who knows?"

The church rose up like a dark mountain in front of them. There was a strong wind blowing that made the scaffolding creak. The churchyard was dark, and Black jumped when a badger ran out in front of them.

"It's only a badger," Blue said.

"Do you think dead people come back to life at night?" Black asked.

"No, that's impossible," Blue said. "Because their muscles don't work anymore."

Brown said nothing, just followed behind Black and Blue as they made their way to the scaffolding.

"Did you hear something?" Black asked.

"No," Blue said.

"Maybe it was the dead people," Black said.

"Impossible," Blue said.

"I think I heard something," Brown whispered.

The noise was coming from up on the scaffolding. The superheroes could hear someone laughing.

"Maybe it's the roof repairers," Blue said.

"I don't think they work at night," Black said. "Maybe there are dead people up on the scaffolding."

"Look," Brown said and pointed at three bikes. The bikes of the minister's son, Anton, and Ruben. They were standing by a ladder that went up onto the scaffolding.

"What are they doing here?" Blue whispered.

"No idea," Black said.

They heard the minister's son shout something and the others laugh.

"Well, that means we can't paint the church after all," Brown said quietly.

"That's not fair," Black said.

"What should we do with the paint?" Blue asked.

The three superheroes looked at each other right as she said it. They were all thinking the same thing. Without saying a word, they began to push the bikes down the hill.

"I know where we can paint them," Black said. "Down by the school."

They pushed the bikes in behind the school wall. Then they flipped open the lid on the big can of blue paint. Soon, their brushes were dripping, and all three bikes had been covered in a thick coat of blue. Even the seat and handlebars were blue.

"Should we push them back to the church?" Blue wondered.

"I don't know," Brown said.

"They can stay here and dry until tomorrow," Black laughed.

When Rusty woke up, he couldn't remember anything for a few seconds. Then it all came flooding back to him: the blue paint, the bikes by the church, and the half-empty can of paint they had hidden in the bushes behind the school. Suddenly, he had a stomachache. He looked at his hands. There was only a little blue under his nails. He had managed to clean the rest off with paint thinner. He went to the bathroom and found some nail clippers. He had to cut his thumbnail right down to the quick. Then, he cleaned it with soap.

His mother was sitting in the kitchen reading the

newspaper. The table was set for breakfast with bread, butter, and jam. She turned the page before taking a sip of coffee and noticed Rusty standing in the doorway.

"Good morning," she said. Then, "My, you look tired. You look like you didn't sleep a wink all night."

"But I did," Rusty said quickly. "I slept like a rock."

Rusty sat down at the table.

"I had such a strange dream," his mother said. "Your grandpa and I were out fishing, like we used to when I was a girl. We each had a bamboo stick, and he played a strange tune that I can't remember on his Chinese pipe. He was always making up new tunes and used to say that they were old songs that the grooms used to sing to their horses in the sixteenth century. But I knew he was just joking. When we were about to start rowing, the boat wasn't on the water anymore, but in the middle of a big pool of blue paint. As if someone had painted a large lake."

Rusty froze.

"Then Grandpa said it was your turn to wish for

something. I have no idea what he meant. Isn't that a strange dream, Rusty?"

Rusty nodded and grabbed a knife, but he didn't reach for the jam. Instead, he sat there looking at the brown bread.

"Is everything all right, Rusty?"

Rusty didn't answer.

"Is everything all right, Rusty?" his mother asked again.

"No," Rusty said. "It's not."

He ran up to his room. He found the paper package that his grandfather had given him, opened it, and looked at the giraffe's ear. He grabbed the watch and ran out into hall, throwing on his jacket. His mother called after him from the kitchen, "You have to have some breakfast before you run out!"

He only had his shoes half on as he bolted out the door. He ran across the road, past his grandfather's rock, along the path, and up the hill to where the planks that had once been the fort lay. They were still scattered all over the place, looking like a wrecked bird's nest. Rusty sat down on a plank. He took the giraffe's ear from one pocket. Then he took the watch from the other. He opened the paper and looked at the shriveled ear. He put the ear to his lips, and his nose filled with a pungent smell. He whispered something into the ear. Whispered the same words, over and over again. He whispered, and as he repeated the same words as quietly as he could, he saw that the watch had started to work again. The second hand was moving, but not like normal. Rather, it was going in the opposite direction. Slowly, slowly, the second hand was moving backward. Rusty hardly dared to breathe

as the hands ticked in reverse. After one full revolution, they stopped. Rusty sat there and stared at the watch in silence. He had stopped whispering. He wrapped up the ear in its paper again and stood up. The sun was shining over the rooftops.

When Rusty got to Grandpa's rock, he could see a police car outside the house. He felt a great, big, heavy knot in his stomach and quickly ducked down and

hid behind the big rock. The grass behind it was wet, and Rusty's knees got damp. He could feel his heart pounding. He took the watch out of his pocket and held it tight in his hand. He took a couple of deep breaths before standing up and walking to the front door.

"There you are," Rusty's father said when he opened the door.

His father was on his way to the kitchen, and his mother was sitting in the living room with a policewoman and a policeman with a big beard. They turned to Rusty when he came in.

"The police have come to see us," Rusty's father said.

"It's about the paint," the policeman said.

Rusty nodded and felt his knees trembling.

"There's been some trouble," his mother said.

Rusty held the watch in his sweaty hand. He held it tight.

"Yes, blue paint," the policewoman said.

Rusty's father came back from the kitchen with cups of coffee for everyone.

"A lot of blue paint has been stolen from Grandpa's garage," his father said.

"It's terrible," his mother said. "Grandpa's just been buried, and then these good-for-nothings come along."

"It's just some boys who got themselves into trouble," the policewoman said. "Boyish pranks, but all the same."

"We've caught them," the policeman said. "Or, rather, they gave themselves away."

"They were covered in blue paint when we found them last night," the policewoman said. "And by then, they had written lots of rude words on the church."

Rusty looked at her and felt his face changing into a big question mark.

"And the minister's son, of all people," his mother said, shaking her head.

"They forced open the garage doors," his father said.

"They said they just wanted to see the vintage car," the policeman explained.

"But forcing open the doors…" his mother started. "They only needed to come and ask…"

"And then they found the paint that we had bought," his father said. "Remember how we were going to paint Grandpa's house this summer, before he got ill?"

Rusty felt empty and strange inside, and it took him a long minute before he could nod naturally.

Rusty rang Lou's doorbell. Her mother opened the door, and the smell of freshly baked raisin buns wafted out. She told Rusty to go straight upstairs. When he stopped outside the door to Lou's room, he heard laughter. He knocked on the door. Lou opened it and burst out laughing as soon as she saw Rusty. Jack was sitting on the bed.

"You're here, too?" Rusty said.

"Lou's granny is just so funny," Jack laughed. "She had a boyfriend once who looked just like a horse. And his surname was Nai-ai-aismith."

Lou exploded with laughter again, and Rusty had to laugh too.

When they had all calmed down, Rusty said,
"Anton, Ruben, and the minister's son have been
caught by the police."

"The police?"

"Apparently, they stole a whole lot of blue paint
from Grandpa's garage. And they wrote lots of rude
words on the church. When the police caught them,
they were covered in blue paint, which was a bit of a
giveaway. Even their bikes were blue."

Lou and Jack started to laugh again.

Lou's mother came in with a tray of fresh raisin buns.

"What are you all laughing about?" she asked.

"Nothing," Lou said.

"Nothing?"

"No, nothing in particular," Rusty said.

"It's just those boys," Lou said. "They won't be bothering us anymore."

"That's good," her mother said and put down the tray.

That night, Rusty was woken by the sensation that he was falling. He had been dreaming. He rubbed his eyes and heard the watch ticking. He got up and looked out of the window. There was a faint glow over the hill. All was quiet. Rusty opened the closet where his Brown disguise was hidden. He picked up the mask and looked at it. Then he put it down again. He pulled on his sweater and pants and tiptoed out into the hall.

He crossed the gravel to the road. On the far side, he could see Grandpa sitting on the rock as usual.

"You haven't been buried yet?" Rusty said.

"No," his grandpa replied. "I slipped out of the coffin at the last minute. I couldn't bear the thought of lying still for so long."

"I didn't know you could do that," Rusty said.

Grandpa chuckled quietly.

"What's happening with your fort?" he asked.

"We've started to rebuild it," Rusty said. "Jack, Lou, and I."

"Maybe you should paint it blue?" Grandpa said, and winked knowingly.

Rusty nodded.

"I'm glad you've got two good friends," Grandpa said.

"And I've got you," said Rusty.

Grandpa said nothing. Then he grew serious and looked at Rusty for a long time. He stroked his hair.

"I'm going to have to move on soon," he said. "There's so much I need to do. I have to make sure the wind is blowing properly, so all the leaves collect in piles that you can wade through. And I need to go down to the lake and lure all the big pike out from the reeds, so they'll bite on your silver bait hook. And that means I can't sit here every evening."

"But I don't want you to go, Grandpa."

"I know. That's why I'm going to live on. Inside the

old watch. Whenever you hear it ticking, that will be my old heart beating and me whispering to you that everything will be all right."

"But I don't want you to go."

"I know," Grandpa said. "But you're a smart boy, Rusty. Everything will be all right."

Grandpa stood up and put his arm around Rusty's shoulders.

"Come on," he said. "Let's go up and have a look at this fort of yours. I must have told you about the time I helped build a skyscraper in America? I'm sure I've got a trick or two to make your fort more solid."

"Really, Grandpa?" Rusty asked.

"Yep, believe me," Grandpa said. "Why wouldn't it be true?"

They walked along the dark path at the back of the gardens up the hill to where some flimsy planks made up the frame of what would become a blue fort at the edge of the forest.

www.enchantedlion.com

Library of Congress Cataloging-in-Publication Data

Names: Øvreås, Håkon, 1974– author. | Torseter, Øyvind, illustrator. |
  Dickson, Kari, translator.
Title: Brown / Håkon Øvreås ; illustrated by Øyvind Torseter ; translated
  from the Norwegian by Kari Dickson.
Other titles: *Brune*. English
Description: New York : Enchanted Lion Books, [2018] | Summary: With help
  from his recently deceased grandfather, new friends and their superhero
  alter egos, and some paint, Rusty stops the bullies who have been
  terrorizing their small town.
Identifiers: LCCN 2018022904| ISBN 9781592702121 (hardcover : alk. paper) |
  ISBN 9781592702510 (pbk. : alk. paper)
Subjects: | CYAC: Bullying--Fiction. | Friendship--Fiction. |
  Superheroes--Fiction. | Family life--Norway--Fiction. | Norway--Fiction.
Classification: LCC PZ7.O9693 Bro 2018 | DDC [E]--dc23
LC record available at https://lccn.loc.gov/2018022904

First English-language edition published in 2019 by Enchanted Lion Books
67 West Street, 317A, Brooklyn, NY 11222
Edited by Claudia Zoe Bedrick and Kate Finney
Originally published in Norway in 2013 as *Brune*
Copyright © 2013 by Gyldendal Norsk Forlag AS
Copyright © 2019 by Enchanted Lion Books for the English-language Translation
All rights reserved under International and Pan-American Copyright Conventions
ISBN: 978-1-59270-212-1 (hardcover) ; 978-1-59270-251-0 (trade paper)

Printed by Worzalla, Stevens Point, WI
Second Printing

Håkon Øvreås is a celebrated poet, with several published collections. *Brown*, his first book for children, has been a smashing success in Norway and has received numerous awards, including the Norwegian Ministry of Culture's Literature Prize. A global best-seller, *Brown* has also been published in at least 32 languages throughout the world.

Øyvind Torseter is an illustrator and cartoonist and one of Norway's most acclaimed cultural figures. He works in both traditional and digital media and has received great recognition and numerous prizes. His books *My Father's Arms Are A Boat* (Batchelder Honor), *The Hole*, *Why Dogs Have Wet Noses*, and *The Heartless Troll* are also available in English from Enchanted Lion Books.

Born in Edinburgh, Scotland, **Kari Dickson** grew up bilingually, speaking English in her daily life and Norwegian with her mother and grandparents. She holds a B.A. in Scandinavian studies and an M.A.in translation.

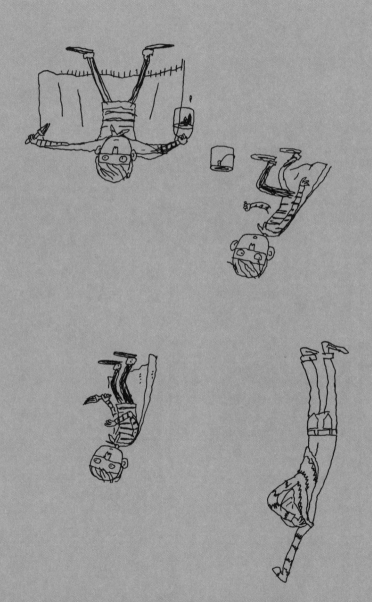